LITTLE HOUSE
Laura Ingalls Wilder

M Y   F I R S T   L I T T L E   H O U S E   B O O K S

Laura's Christmas

JHOL
Wilde

Laura's Christmas

ADAP...   S

It's Christmastime in the Big Woods
and the little house is buried in snow.
Where is Laura?

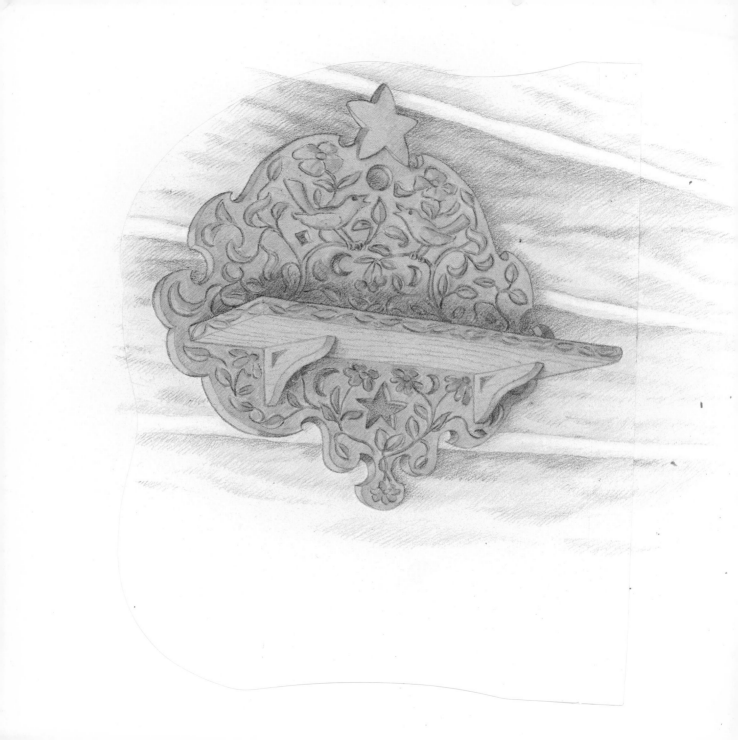

Pa built Ma a wooden shelf
for Christmas.

What is on it?

Ma bakes cookies for Christmas.
What special treat do Laura and Mary get?

What game do Laura and Mary play in the snow?

It's Christmas Eve and time for bed.
Who is still awake?

What do Laura and Mary find in their stockings on Christmas morning?

What special present did Santa bring for Laura?

What a merry Christmas!